For Mailee and her grandchildren — J.O.
For Jason x — Lindsey

OXFORD
UNIVERSITY PRESS

Great Clarendon Street, Oxford OX2 6DP
Oxford University Press is a department of the University of Oxford.
It furthers the University's objective of excellence in research, scholarship,
and education by publishing worldwide in

Oxford   New York

Auckland   Cape Town   Dar es Salaam   Hong Kong   Karachi
Kuala Lumpur   Madrid   Melbourne   Mexico City   Nairobi
New Delhi   Shanghai   Taipei   Toronto

With offices in

Argentina   Austria   Brazil   Chile   Czech Republic   France   Greece
Guatemala   Hungary   Italy   Japan   Poland   Portugal   Singapore
South Korea   Switzerland   Thailand   Turkey   Ukraine   Vietnam

Oxford is a registered trade mark of Oxford University Press
in the UK and in certain other countries

British Library Cataloguing in Publication

Data available

ISBN: 978-0-19-279170-2 (Hardback)
ISBN: 978-0-19-279171-9 (Paperback)
ISBN: 978-0-19-279246-4 (Paperback with audio CD)

1 3 5 7 9 10 8 6 4 2

Printed in China

Paper used in the production of this book is a natural,
recyclable product made from wood grown in sustainable forests.
The manufacturing process conforms to the environmental
regulations of the country of origin.

Over in the Clover

Jan
Ormerod

OXFORD
UNIVERSITY PRESS

Lindsey
Gardiner

Over in the **forest**, in a cave so **snug**,
one cubby bear gives his mummy a **hug**.

'Hug!' says the mummy.
'I hug!' says the one.
And they snuggle, buggle, hug
in their cave so snug.

Over in the **jungle**, in a **leafy** glade,
two stripy tigers **tumble** in the shade.

'Roll!' says the daddy.

'We roll!' say the two.

And they jungle, bungle, tumble
in their shady glade.

Over in the clover, in the bright moonlight,
three baby moles burrow through the night.

'Dig!' says the mummy.

'We dig!' say the three.

And they **doggle, daggle, dig** in the **bright** moonlight.

Over by the river,
at the trunk of a tree,
four busy beavers
chew noisily.

'Gnash!' says the daddy.
'We gnash!' say the four.

And they gnash, crash, splash!

at the trunk of the tree.

Over in the clouds, on a mountain crest,
six fluffy eagles **flap** in a nest.

'Flap!' says the daddy.
'We flap!' say the six.

And they
flip,
flap,
fly
from
their nest
on a crest.

Over in the desert, by a dusty pool, **seven** little warthogs try to keep **cool**.

'Snuffle!' says the mummy.

'We snuffle!' say the seven.

And they shuffle, wuffle, snuffle by the dusty pool.

Over in the garden,
where it's lovely and warm,

eight pretty kitties
s t r e t c h
paws on the lawn.

'Stretch!' says the daddy.
'We stretch!'
say the eight.

And
they
furry, purry,
s t r e t c h

on the
lawn in the
warm.

Over in the park, on a grassy mound, **nine** puppy dogs chase round and round.

Over in the **fishpond**,
underneath
a log,

ten tiny tadpoles
waiting to be frogs!

'Wiggle!'
says the daddy.

'We wiggle!'
say the ten.

And they wiggle, waggle, woggle
underneath a log, and wiggle into . . .

frogs!

1 one cubby bear

2 two stripy tigers

3 three baby moles

4 four busy beavers

5 five kangaroos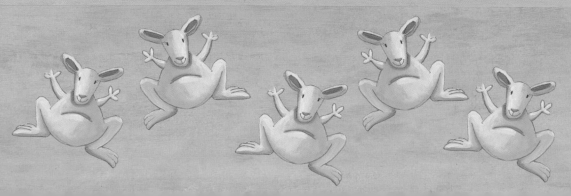

6   six fluffy eagles

7   seven little warthogs

8   eight pretty kitties

9   nine puppy dogs

10   ten tiny tadpoles